SANTA COW ISLAND

SANTA COW ISLAND

By
Cooper Edens

Illustrated by
Daniel Lane

ALADDIN PAPERBACKS

First Aladdin Paperbacks edition October 1999

Text copyright © 1994 by Cooper Edens
Illustrations copyright © 1994 by Daniel Lane

Aladdin Paperbacks
An imprint of Simon & Schuster Children's Publishing Division
1230 Avenue of the Americas
New York, NY 10020

Also available in a Simon & Schuster Books for Young Readers hardcover edition.
Designed by Paul Zakris
The text for this book was set in 14-point Kabel Bold.
The illustrations were rendered in watercolor, accompanied by pen and ink.

Printed in Hong Kong
10 9 8 7 6 5 4 3 2 1

The Library of Congress has cataloged the hardcover edition as follows:
Edens, Cooper.
Santa Cow Island / by Cooper Edens ;
illustrated by Daniel Lane.
p.   cm.
Summary: Mounted on the flying Santa Cows, the Schwartzes travel
to the South Seas for New Year's vacation.
[1. Cows—Fiction. 2. Oceania—Fiction. 3. Vacations—Fiction.
4. New Year—Fiction. 5. Stories in rhyme.]
I. Lane, Daniel, ill. II. Title.
PZ8.3.E21295Sal   1994   [E]—dc20   93-30899   CIP   AC
ISBN 0-671-88319-4 (hc.)
ISBN 0-689-82869-1 (pbk.)

For Alan Benjamin
—C. E.

For Alexis,
with special thanks to C. T.
—D. L.

Twas the day after Christmas; warmer climes were my wish,

So I asked the dear Cows if they thought me foolish.

"Not at all," they replied. "And here's an invitation:

Come fly with us now for a Cow Isle Vacation."

I shared with the family the Cows' slick brochure.

They went wild when they saw "South Sea Cow Adventure."

I said, "Where we're going it's sunny and bright,

But you must be patient; it's a very long flight."

Then we swung ourselves up on the Cows' sturdy backs,
First cramming some snack foods inside our knapsacks.
We rose high o'er the Hudson as we started our quest,
Circled the Great Lady, and at Newark turned west.

O'er Pittsburgh and Cleveland the sight from below

Was as grand, I am sure, as a Michelangelo.

High above St. Louis, checking compasses in flight,

The Cows changed our course *one point five* hooves to the right.

On to California our joyful herd flew.

We traveled full speed as the westerlies blew.

We held fast to our mounts as each Cow deftly steered.

O'er the Golden Gate Bridge like shooting stars we appeared.

Next day we were stunt pilots over Ocean Pacific,

Executing spins both daring and prolific,

When straight down we saw spelled in tight Cow formation:

"Welcome, dear Schwartzes, to your New Year's vacation."

On Santa Cow Island our very first day,

The Cows taught me to surf the quadruped way.

While Elwood submerged in the clear coral reef,

The kids inhaled Chee-tos, but swore off dried beef.

At midday we challenged the Cows to mixed doubles,

But suffered from sunburn and double-fault troubles.

While the Cows' play was flawless (they served only aces),

Poor Elwood and I—the balls flew past our faces.

Then, as the sun set on the tropical scene,

We went with the Cows into that ocean so green.

'Twas the ultimate thrill: outrigger canoeing,

With Schwartzes and Cows bonding, chanting, and mooing.

Next morning the Holsteins, on the isle's scenic coast,
Threw a party at poolside with S'mores we could toast.
They amazed our whole family with high-diving feats
Like "A Full Cowabunga with High-Flying Teats."

Then 'twas off with the Cows to play golf—eighteen holes.

We drove like Al Unser and made divots like moles.

The Cows showed my Elwood the best club for each "lie,"

'Specially how to chip off a Santa Cow pie.

We were back on the beach on our very last day
For volleyball action; everyone wanted to play.
It was Shirts versus Skins; yes, Schwartz against Cow,
And though they stayed earthbound, they still spiked us somehow.

Then we all wandered off to find pastimes to please,
To chew cuds or Milk Duds under shady palm trees,
Or to dip with the dolphin; just imagine the fun!
Happiest was Dex, our pizza-guy son.

At last came New Year's Eve, a most gala occasion
With milkshakes, Liz Taylor, and much jubilation.
The Cows in black tie and in chorus of mirth
Cheered a Happy New Year, and for all Peace on Earth.

PEACE ON EARTH